Cosy Burrow Books

VALKYRIE ACADEMY DRAGON ALLIANCE
Book Ten

DECEIVED

"Kara and the dragons fight to save Asgard in this action-packed book! Fans of the series can look forward to exciting revelations during the battle." Kristina B., Proofreader, Red Adept Editing

VALKYRIE ACADEMY DRAGON ALLIANCE BOOKS

MARKED (PREQUEL)
CHOSEN
VANISHED
SCORNED
INFLICTED
EMPOWERED
AMBUSHED
WARNED
ABDUCTED
BESIEGED
DECEIVED

Cosy Burrow Books

VALKYRIE ACADEMY DRAGON ALLIANCE

DECEIVED

KATRINA COPE

Deceived
Ebook first published in USA in January 2020 by Cosy
Burrow Books
Ebook first published in Great Britain in January 2020
by Cosy Burrow Books

www.katrinacopebooks.com
Text Copyright © 2019 by Katrina Cope
Cover Design Copyright © art4artists.com.au
The moral right of Katrina Cope to be identified as the
author of this work has been asserted
All rights reserved
No part of this publication may be reproduced or
transmitted by any means, electronic, mechanical,
photocopying or otherwise, without the prior permission
of the publisher

This book is a work of fiction. Any references or
suggestions herein to actual historical events, real people
or actual locations are fictitious. All names,
characterisations, locations, incidents, and fabrications
are solely the product of the author's imagination, and
any, and all, resemblance to actual persons alive or dead
or locations or events is entirely coincidental.
Published by Cosy Burrow Books
All rights reserved

ISBN: 978-0-6486613-9-9

Michael ~ your support means the world to me

Would you like a FREE copy of Marked?
Visit here:
https://www.katrinacopebooks.com/valkyrie-academy-dragon-alliance
Through this link you can sign up for my newsletter and receive a FREE copy of Marked plus updates about my fantasy books, sales and notification of giveaways.

- CHAPTER ONE -

I charge forward, a war cry bursting from my mouth. Asgard is my home. Whether it has welcomed me with open arms or not, it is my home, and I'm not going to let it fall. One of my best friends, Eir, is missing. Hildr, Britta, and Naga are hurt, but I am not going to give up. I'll fight for them, Asgard, and myself. How dare these dark elves invade my home and try to take over Odin's palace?

With my sword in hand and magic swirling at my fingertips, I'm ready to fight. As I charge toward the battlefield, I hear a cry off to the side. I turn to find one of the finest warriors from our reaped souls being overpowered by a dark elf. The warrior's side is slashed open. He attempts to hold the wound together with his hands, which leaves him defenseless. I release all of my built-up magic, shooting it at the elf. Unaware of my presence and taken off guard, the dark elf careens sideways and collides into another dark elf. The surprised look on their faces remains as they regroup their focus.

I charge to the warrior and help him off the battlefield. "You're no good to us like this. Can you make it to the healer on your own?"

The warrior nods and slowly staggers in the direction of the castle. When I return my attention to the battle, the elf I knocked down has risen to his feet. Swinging my sword, I approach him, only to find my blow blocked before I connect. I swipe my sword down the elf's and spin, swiping the sword horizontally at his torso. He pushes his rear end back, narrowly missing the sword tip as it swings past his abdomen. At the same time, he swipes his sword in the opposite direction, aiming for my neck. I pull back just in time, feeling the slightest cut as the sword drags across my skin. Fear envelops me, and I'm tempted to throw a hand up to my neck. It doesn't feel vital, so I pull my thoughts together and send out a stream of magic. He raises his hand and creates a barrier. The magic bounces off, hitting the dirt below and causing it to scatter, creating a small crater.

Using his other hand, the elf swings his sword again, aiming at my torso. I bend my knees and push off my toes, springing just out of reach of the sword's tip. In the same movement, I swiftly launch forward and kick out, landing a side kick into the dark elf's unguarded stomach. The force knocks him back a couple of meters, and a startled look appears on his face.

As he tries to recoup, I charge forward, aiming my sword directly at his heart. At the last second, he flings his arm out. His sword knocks my aim aside as he twists out of the way, then he punches me in the face with the hilt. My head throbs with pain, and my eyes won't focus, making it hard to pull my thoughts together.

Something hot burns down my right shoulder to my torso, and I scream. Automatically, my left hand reaches for the wound, and I cringe when I feel the deep cut. Blood covers my hand. I grit my teeth and look down. Thanks to my sturdy leather, the wound is not too deep. Still, the dark elf has cut down my side. The elven blade is well-made and sharper than most.

The elf swings again while I'm distracted, and I manage to dodge the blow, but my feet catch on a rock. I stumble to the ground, landing flat on my back. He lunges forward and stands steadily above me. He raises his sword, ready to plummet it straight into my heart.

It takes all of my energy to gather enough magic, but I use what I have to attempt to force the sword aside. Somehow the dark elf manages to hold it straight. The tip inches closer to my body. A sneer decorates the elf's face as he measures his success. My energy drains quickly, and I'm afraid that I won't be able to hold him off much longer.

Suddenly, he's knocked aside. A flash of white passes over me, and a battle takes place in front of my eyes. The elf cries out in pain as a blond Valkyrie attacks with the expertise of someone who has had years of practice. She knocks him aside so fast that he doesn't have time to gather his magic and struggles to raise his sword. The Valkyrie swings left then right, dodging the elf's blows, missing his attacks, and managing to nick him in spots where he has left his guard down.

My vision clears slightly, and I gaze at her face. "Rota?"

She ignores me and continues her battle—one-hundred percent focused on the dark elf. Only moments pass before she swings the final blow of her sword straight into his heart. Even with all his magic powers, he was unable to stop her attack.

Looking satisfied with the outcome, Rota hunkers down and yanks the sword out of his chest before wiping it against the dark elf's clothes. She gazes over at me with a triumphant look on her face.

"Thank you," I say as I push myself up on my elbows, still in shock that Rota came to save me.

"It's about time I got to pay you back. You fight well for someone who hasn't had much practice, but you still have a long way to go." She walks over, reaches out a hand, and pulls me up. Then she gazes at my shoulder and down my torso. "The cut is not too deep."

Absentmindedly, I touch the wound and wince.

A slight hint of sympathy crosses Rota's face. "Although I'm sure it hurts. Are you all right to keep going?"

"Yes. Thanks again."

She nods once then spins to look for the next dark elf to battle, giving me a glimpse of her blood-splattered white wings. Judging by the lack of wounds on her body, it's a relief to know that not any of it is hers.

Glancing again at my shoulder and torso, I realize that she's right. It's not that deep, and since I'm a Valkyrie, it will heal quickly.

I take a moment to deal with the pain and stand back to watch the fight. Several senior Valkyries and warriors have been slain and, thankfully, some dark elves with them. Drogon and Tanda continue to fly above, flicking aside enemies when they come too close, and shooting fire when the opportunity arises. They manage to set several elves alight.

The angels of death continue to fight alongside the Valkyries, showing a scattered array of black and white wings. Two enemies fighting on the same side is a welcome sight. I'm still unable to find Harut, which leaves worry gnawing my stomach. I haven't seen him since before I went searching for the warriors.

A warm female voice sounds from behind me. "It's nice to see this, isn't it? To see the angels of death and the Valkyries fighting together." Freya stands a few feet behind me, her eyes scanning the battlefield. "I'm so glad you called me. It was the right choice. Your fierce-hearted warriors don't have the talent to fight against the dark elves. They don't stand a chance against their magic. They don't seem to understand it. Even though they are good at what they do, you need more power than what they can bring."

"What about your angels of death? Are they used to fighting against magic?"

"Undoubtedly, they have more experience than your warriors. I still wouldn't class them as competent against magic. It's not something they have. They have the reaping powers of the winged Valkyries but not the power of magic."

I survey the field again, my eyes continually searching. My heartbeat speeds up with anticipation. "Have you seen Harut? I can't see him anywhere."

Her eyes hold understanding as she looks at me and smiles. "Oh, child, Harut is not all that he seems."

"What do you mean?"

"He is not a true angel of death. He is a soul unto his own."

"I still don't understand. He's always been there, helping reap souls for Folkvanger, and he's always been kind to me."

"Let's just say he comes and goes as he pleases. I'm not sure where his loyalty lies. He

is a strange one, even for an angel of death."
Her voice is peaceful and calm as she says this.
I study the fields for a few minutes longer,
giving my wounds more time to heal. I'm not
comfortable with the way things look. The
Valkyries and angels of death still struggle to
fight against the dark elves and keep the battle
even. At the same time, my mind puzzles over
what Freya means about Harut.

A clang of metal sounds behind me, and my
shoulders turn numb. *That is awfully close.*

- CHAPTER TWO -

I turn, panic gripping my core. I'd let my guard down… again. I was too distracted by Rota saving me and by Harut missing. My heart pumps wildly, and my eyes widen, ready to fight, only to face Britta.

She spins around and clashes her sword against the female elf's and uses her other hand to shoot magic, blasting the dark elf several feet away. The female elf is quick on her feet and balances before charging back at Britta. It is the first female dark elf I have seen fighting, although she is just as aggressive as the male elves. I gather my magic as I watch Britta brace herself for the clash. I shout and blast the elf sideways into another group of fighters.

An Einherji warrior in the group spots the female elf flying toward him, and he kicks his own elf backward. At the same time, he moves with precision, aiming his sword directly at the incoming female elf. His blade pierces straight into her heart. The warrior retrieves his sword and continues fighting his dark elf as though the female elf never existed.

Now that our elf is taken care of, I gaze at Britta's leg. It's straight again, but as she walks, she seems to be favoring it.

"What are you doing here?" I indicate her leg. "Your leg was broken."

Britta grins. "That's the beauty of being a Valkyrie. Anita smeared it with her special salve and reset it before securing it in a splint.

With our Valkyrie healing power and her expertise, it almost feels as good as new." She paces with a limp as if to prove a point.

"Yeah, *almost* like new," I say sarcastically. "You should be resting."

"I can't rest while I know Asgard is under attack. I'm not the only one. Even though Hildr had some major injuries, she should be back soon too. We are both keen to finish this war so we can look for Eir." She gnaws at her lip and frowns. "I really hope she's okay."

My heart sinks, remembering the disappearance of our friend. "Me too. Did Naga make it to Anita?"

"Yes. She's working on him now. I don't know if he will make it back before the war finishes, though. Dragons don't have healing powers like the Valkyries."

A cry sounds, and I turn around in time to see a dark elf being ripped away only a couple of feet from us. An invisible force flings her sideways.

"Thank you, Elan," I call into the air.

You're welcome. I'm not going to let some dark elf attack you, but you've got to stop letting your guard down. You need to be more careful.

"She's right." Britta grips her sword, her knuckles turning white, and spins to fight. She flicks her other hand and shoots magic at a dark elf that was fighting an Einherji. The elf is flung sideways, uncornering the soul-reaped warrior.

The Einherji spins to her and mutters a brief thanks before chasing after the dark elf with his sword held high, ready to take the plunge. Seeing her do this makes me glad that the zmey marked my friends with magic. So far, the battle is not looking great for us, but it would look a lot worse if we didn't have any magic on our side.

I hear the sound of exerted effort and turn around to spot Cael struggling to fight off the leader of the dark elves. Both the angel of death and the dark elf are over six feet tall with muscle-bound frames. Cael has the advantage of wings, and the dark elf has the power of magic, not a good match even though both are skilled fighters.

Cael beats off the dark elf. If it weren't for the chief dark elf's magic, Cael would be doing a lot better. Instead, the magic that the dark elf holds is causing him all sorts of problems. I shoot magic at the dark elves' leader, but he doesn't budge. He's cornering Cael. Even though the angel of death isn't the warmest of personalities toward me, he's fighting for our side. He's not a warrior that we would like to lose.

My magic bounces off the chief dark elf's barrier. I get the impression that he must have felt it because he glances sideways. A sly smile spreads across his face, and his eyes start to search until, finally, they land on me. He focuses back on Cael, drawing his sword and swiping it. He knocks Cael's sword from his hand then raises his sword for the deep plunge.

Cael scurries back and stumbles, falling to the ground. Rapidly, he retreats, crawling backward like a crab.

I shoot magic at the chief dark elf again, and it bounces off. I curse under my breath. I have to think of something new. Then an idea occurs to me. I shoot more magic, but this time, I shoot a barrier designed to block all weapons between Cael and the dark elf leader. I sense it lingering in front of Cael as he continues to scramble backward, not knowing what I've done.

The chief dark elf stomps after Cael, his sword raised high. That horrid smirk remains on the dark elf's face, and I long to wipe it off. It's frustrating knowing none of my magic will touch him. The dark elf doesn't even look injured from my attacks on him earlier. The blood from his earlier wound is dried and caked to his cloak. Sure-footed, he continues his pursuit of Cael.

I continue to hold my magic barrier in front of Cael. *This has to protect him.* At the same time, I try to concentrate on what is going on around me as I need to protect myself too.

A gush of wind sweeps behind me, followed by a thump as Elan snatches another dark elf from sneaking up behind me. I turn back right as the dark elf thrusts his sword toward Cael, aiming straight for his heart. Pushing aside the dread, I mantra to myself, "I've got this. I know I've got this." I watch with confidence that shatters as the dark elf's sword pierces straight through the barrier and into Cael's heart.

My eyes widen as Cael's head drops to the ground and his body slumps. The sword protrudes from his chest and pins him in place. His head tilts to the side, and his eyes land on me as the glassy glaze starts to set in.

"No!" I cry, hitting my chest with my fist. I don't understand what happened. With an open mouth, I stare at the chief of the dark elves.

His eyes glint with mischief and satisfaction as he observes me. "Don't you know your magic doesn't stop elven swords? I've blessed each of our weapons with magic. They will pierce through any of your barriers."

Rage and grief make me want to run forward and tear his heart out. I squint, and my feet charge one in front of the other as I draw my sword, ready to end him. To fight well, I must keep my anger in check. It is going to be hard, but my fury is something I have to tame. This war has to stop.

There is so much about the dark elves we haven't learned. There needs to be some changes in the Valkyries' training. The academy has focused too much on fighting angels of death on Midgard, not on the other dangers that threaten Asgard.

The dark elf pulls his sword out of Cael's chest. He wipes the blood on Cael's clothes then holds the sword casually. His eyes are mocking and full of confidence as he stands with his feet in ready stance, watching me approach.

- CHAPTER THREE -

Expelling a war cry, I release my pent-up aggression and charge with my sword held high. The sneer on the dark elf's face, along with the image of glass-eyed Cael, drives me onward. The leader of the dark elf doesn't look ready to fight back, or he is taunting me, standing still because he knows I can't win. I push this negative thought aside. I know I'm not that bad of a fighter, but when I'm only a few feet away, the elf disappears, leaving me standing there, lost in my astonishment. Now I understand why he looked so confident.

I scream into the air. "Coward!"

Checking around me for other dangers, I run to Cael and check his carotid artery. I feel nothing. There isn't a hint of a pulse.

With a heavy heart, I lift him by the armpits and pull him away from being trampled. A deep wailing fills the air, and I turn around to spot Freya coming from the direction of the palace. Tears stream down her flawless face.

Even in her distress, her gracious hips sway as she hastily makes her way to Cael, ignoring the fighting around her. She sinks to the ground, scooping his head in her lap, and strokes his cheek, expressing genuine distress. I'm overwhelmed with disbelief as she caresses him as though he is one of her very own children. I'm not quite sure what to think.

Mistress Sigrun and Odin haven't displayed sympathy or anything close to it. I haven't seen them express any emotion when a Valkyrie has fallen. They have often shrugged it off and moved on.

Seeing the strange array of affection reminds me of Harut. I search through the angels of death, trying to spot him. I come across a figure with gorgeous white wings, lying on the ground. Blood pours out of her side, staining the tan leather jacket and pooling on the soil. It takes me a moment to realize it is Prima. Without a sneer distorting her face, she looks so different and pretty. Pushing aside all animosity, I jog to her side. Unlike Cael, nobody is crying or fussing over her.

"Prima. Can I help you?"

"There is no help for me, wingless." Pain taints her voice and mixes with the spite that I recognize as a desperate attempt to stay strong. "Why would you want to help me?" She lifts her head slightly to focus on me and winces. "And how are you not dead yet? These are excellent fighters, and we are all struggling to fight against them. You haven't had as much training as us."

I squat down by her side. "You're right. I am still going strong thanks to a combination of magic and good luck mixed with a determination that exceeds anyone else's."

She huffs then clasps her side, grimacing.

I catch a glimpse under her hand. A massive gash runs along the side of her abdomen. It is so big, I can see some of her insides. She needs medical attention immediately. I get my bearings and realize that the best path to the healer is through the battlefield. The academy is on the other side of the dark elves.

A warm flush runs up the side of my arm. I glance over to see Drogon spewing fire at a group of dark elves. The dark elves dodge to the side, limiting the hit of the direct flame, and I curse their quick reflexes.

When the flame stops, I call to the dragon. "Drogon!" He bats his wings, lifting him higher, and I call out again. "Drogon!"

His horny head tilts sideways as he gazes down at me. His eyes catch sight of Prima, and he snorts, shooting steam out of his nostrils.

His voice fills my head, tainted with hostility. *Yes?*

"Can you please take Prima to Anita?"

Why would I want to do that? His brown eyes are sharp as he gazes over her. *And more to the point, why would you want to do that?*

"I understand your hostility, Drogon. I know she's one of the winged ones that mistreated your kind and possibly you in the early days. But please, take her to the healer. Things have got to change in Asgard, and this is another step in the right direction."

A muffled groan comes out of his massive form, but he veers to the side and lands not far from us. He takes a quick look at Prima's side and snorts, pushing more steam out of his nostrils. *If she sits up, her insides might come out. I think it's best if I take her in my talons.*

"Thank you, Drogon."

He nods once and scoops Prima into his talons with extraordinary gentleness.

Prima's eyes fill with panic, and I clasp her hand. "Relax. He's taking you to Anita. He won't hurt you. He promised," I lie, but I'm confident that Drogon won't hurt her this time. Some of the tension melts from her body, and her eyes slowly close. Drogon unfurls his wings and takes to the sky with Prima's bloodied wings drooping from his talons.

I watch for the briefest second as the dragon takes her away. Then I pull myself back to reality. Not far from me, swords clash continuously, and I feel the exhaustion settling in. My muscles are battle-weary, and I'm tired of hearing the sounds of fighting. I can only imagine how others feel, especially the winged Valkyries. Even though they are seasoned fighters, this experience is on a completely different level than a small battle over a soul from Midgard. Rarely does the fight between an angel of death and a Valkyrie end with one of them dying—injured maybe, but rarely anything more. This battle is for life, death, and the protection of Asgard.

With a thirst for death on their faces, the dark elves pursue their goal relentlessly, slowly inching their way closer to the palace. We could certainly use the help of Loki and his army. Even help from Thor, the god of thunder, wouldn't go astray right now.

As I stand back, observing the area and letting my muscles recoup, my eyes land on Freya, her body still rocking with sobs. I remember that she came from the palace a short time ago.

"Freya. I'm sorry to interrupt your mourning, but did you see Loki or Thor at the palace when you were there?"

It takes a moment for her to pull her face away from Cael. Her cheeks are lined with tears, and her beautiful blue eyes are rimmed with a red puffiness. Cael's head remains resting in Freya's lap, and her hand runs absentmindedly over his long dark-brown hair, caressing him as though he's a long-lost love.

She shakes her head, her long blond locks brushing Cael's still face. "No. I didn't see any of them. Odin is still up there under the protection of his guards. He is furious over the war, but his warriors won't let him out. Heimdall demanded that he stay. I believe Thor is busy on Midgard with Jormungand."

"The Midgard serpent?"

She nods, and a shiver runs down my spine. "If Thor is battling the Midgard serpent, then isn't this Ragnarök?"

She wipes a tear from her cheek and shrugs. "Possibly. The predictions are never one-hundred-percent correct, and they can be changed. The future is never fixed." She wipes the tears from the other side of her face with her sleeve. "And interpretations of the predictions are just that—interpretations."

"Thank you, Freya."

She nods and turns back to Cael. Her noisy sobs continue. If she mourns one angel of death like this, I would hate to imagine what she would be like if she lost several more. Suddenly she cries out, "This war must stop. We can't lose any more of our precious warriors. There must be another way or someone else we can call on."

Guilt churns deep in my stomach. I haven't been completely honest with Freya, yet she has been consistently kind to me. She even came when I called her to help save Asgard. Now she's crying over one of her fallen senior angels of death. My hands turn numb. I almost feel helpless because of the truth that I've withheld from her. It feels like a betrayal.

I can't watch any longer. "Freya, I know you said Thor was battling the Midgard serpent, but are you sure you haven't seen Loki?"

She nods her head.

I shuffle my feet awkwardly. "There's something I haven't told you yet. When you asked me about this secret army, I didn't disclose to you who it was. I had just found out not long before you asked me, but I withheld the information because I had only just met you, and I didn't know who to trust."

Freya's tearstained face looks up at me, her expression full of expectation.

"The other army is organized by Loki. He has raised an army of dwarf giants and dragons, and he has set up base on Jotunheim."

Not knowing how to deal with her silence, I look back at the battlefield and watch the combat. The battle is close to even in strength. Our numbers far outweigh the dark elves, but we don't have the magic that they have.

I turn back to Freya. "He said he was raising it to protect Asgard, but I don't know why he's not here. Surely he must know by now that we need his help."

Freya's shoulders slump some more, and she sighs loudly. "I should have known." She strokes the long black strands of Cael's hair. Her face is deep in thought. "You need to find Harut."

"Why?"

"Because he knows more than he's letting on. He isn't a true member of the angels of death. I have let him pose as one because I have a large heart, yet I was watching him closely. I feel there is much he is withholding from me. It's one of the reasons why I called you in. From what I heard, I knew that you would be honest with me and that your heart is pure. I also knew that you had a subtle connection with Harut. For some reason, he's been watching you. I need you to find him and see what you can find out from him."

My head spins in confusion. I always thought that Harut was just a nice guy. I have to put this confusion to rest and find out the answers. "I will." I place a hand on the back of her shoulder, trying to offer some form of comfort. Then I leave her to work through her grief.

As I spin away, I think I see Harut in the distance, walking in the opposite direction. I call out to him. "Harut!" He continues as though oblivious to me calling his name. I run toward him and call again. "Harut!"

He seems to pause for a moment and glance over his shoulder. Between his wings, I think I see his eyes land on me and a smile form on his face, but then he continues forward. I must have imagined it.

- CHAPTER FOUR -

I don't understand. Harut isn't fighting, and he didn't stop when I called him. I'm certain that he heard me. The confusion is overwhelming, and my curiosity overtakes me. I run after him, trying to catch up, but he manages to keep several paces ahead of me.

As I rush forward, I'm surrounded by numerous thuds. I glance about to see arrow shafts poking out of the ground in a semicircle around me. I follow the direction of the shafts to find a dark elf standing on top of a mountain, his bow pointing in my direction. I curse under my breath. I should've grabbed my cloak off Elan's back. All the dragon scales work like a shield and would protect me from swords and arrows. I duck sideways, tucking in along the nearby mountain and trying to blend in to the shadow.

Increasing my pace, I try to catch up to Harut, but the time spent dodging arrows has put me farther behind. Several thuds sound again, and numerous arrows embed into the ground in front of me, blocking my path. I'm surprised that no arrows have landed behind me. The dark elf has to be an expert marksman. I don't understand why he's shooting the arrows in front of me rather than behind me or at me. It's almost as though the elf is blocking my path to Harut on purpose. He can't be miscalculating, especially when the first lot of arrows were much closer.

I dart around the shafts and progress forward. A cry of pain assaults my ears, and I pause, searching for the owner of the scream.

Mist stumbles backward, a shaft sticking out of her shoulder. "Blasted Vanir! This is going to leave a scar on my shoulder."

I move to help her, knowing that she will be unable to fight with an injured arm.

Mist swaps the sword into her other hand and presses forward, swinging it at the dark elf in front of her. "You wretched dark elves. You deserve to die, and I'm going to be the one that does it."

She looks like she has things under control, so I continue my pursuit of Harut. At first, I panic, thinking I have lost him, then a flash of dark wings disappears around the side of the mountain. I dig in my toes and charge forward, keeping one eye on the sniper on the mountain. I see him nock another arrow, and when he releases it, several arrowheads fly my way. I've never seen a shaft capable of shooting many arrows at once.

I retrieve my bow off my back and retaliate by shooting one arrow directly at him while running. A split second later, he releases his arrow, this time aiming straight at me. I use my last bit of strength to increase my speed, trying to avoid being hit. At the same time, I glance over my shoulder, watching my own arrow aim directly at him. Its aim is true, and the arrow hits him directly in the chest. He flops backward, and I turn in time to see one of his arrows heading straight in front of me. If I run any faster, I'll be running right into them.

I dodge around the arrows he just shot, chasing the direction of Harut as I watch for any movement. I glance back at the dark elf. He doesn't rise again, so I concentrate on my search for Harut. I haven't spotted him in a little while.

Continuing my search, I run forward only to stop when another group of arrows thuds around me. I thought I had knocked the elf out. Before I can search the mountaintop, a cry of pain rings out. Instinctively, I glance toward the noise and spot Mistress Sigrun. She is keeled over with an arrow shaft sticking out of her stomach. Her hands are embracing the shaft as though this will take away the pain. She groans and collapses to the ground.

A dark elf charges directly at her, his sword raised high. I shoot him with my magic, knocking him aside, but he gets up and charges forward again.

I grunt in frustration. These elves never seem to die. I release more of my welled magic, throwing my arm forward from the shoulder. I use the added force and shoot magic directly at the dark elf. He topples back several feet from Mistress Sigrun, bumping into an angel of death. Instantly, the angel of death sees the elf as his next opponent.

I grab the mistress and rest her head on my lap as I observe the arrow shaft sticking out of her stomach.

"Leave me, wingless." The mistress's blue eyes tighten with pain. "Go and fight. I'll be fine."

"That's not going to happen, Mistress. You need help."

Feeling helpless, my fingers fiddle with the edges of her tan jacket as I think how impractical this uniform is for a battle maiden. Black leathers would've been a better choice.

More arrows thud around us, and I glance up to see Tanda swoop down and attack the dark elf on top of the mountain. I mustn't have hit him with a fatal blow. Tanda captures him in her mouth and gives him a shake before tossing him over the edge of the cliff.

She dives toward a group of elves on the ground, several feet away from me, and I call, "Tanda!"

Her dive doesn't falter, but her red eyes glance to the side and focus on me. Then she looks at the mistress before her nose screws up into a snarl. She finishes her dive, managing to grab one of the elves. Then she shakes him and tosses him aside. Her red eyes burn with hatred as she glances back at me holding the mistress.

"I know. I know. You hate this mistress with a passion. But please, please take her to the healer."

Tanda's eyes harden as she glares at the mistress again. She snorts out a stream of steam toward the mistress, and my face warms as it narrowly misses me. Tanda flicks her tail then dives at the group of elves again, shooting a plume of fire at them and releasing all her pent-up aggression from seeing the mistress.

She circles around and down at me again. *If I had the choice, I would have wished that she was on the receiving end of that attack.*

"I can only imagine that seeing the mistress's face is what created a flame as long and intense as the one you just released."

You have no idea.

"I know you received nothing but mistreatment from her, Tanda. I know she deserves every bit of punishment from what she has done to you and other dragons. But please—for the sake of Asgard and the peace between dragons and the Valkyries, winged or wingless—please take her to the healer. Each time one of the dragons helps the Valkyries out is another sign that you shouldn't be fighting each other."

Tanda flaps her wings, lifting her higher, and circles the area. Her silence is cutting, and for a moment, I think she's going in the other direction.

"Please, Tanda. Please do this. I can feel your pain, and I understand. But please?"

She flicks her head to the side and shoots more steam out of her nostrils. Then slowly, she lowers.

I guess so. Can I carry her in my stomach and throw her up later?

Despite everything, I can't help but smirk. "That's an interesting idea, Tanda, but I don't think it will be the best way to keep the arrow shaft from wedging deeper and causing more damage."

She lands then stomps her feet and lowers her front. I help Mistress Sigrun onto the saddle, and Tanda shoots fire on the dark elves approaching.

I hook the mistress's feet into the stirrups and hand her the reins. "I hope you remember this. Tanda hates you, yet she's still helping you because it's the right thing to do and because I asked her to."

The mistress sits silently, gazing at me with hazy eyes. I move around to the front of

Tanda's nose and rub it gently. "Thank you, Tanda."

She nods then takes to the sky.

I continue my search, reaching the edge of the mountain, and turn the corner. I halt when I see something far in the distance. It isn't the black wings of Harut I expected to find. Instead, down the far end of the mountain, I see a dark elf facing my direction. Standing in front of him is a small bald figure. They appear to be deep in conversation.

I can't believe my eyes. I move several steps closer and call, "Gilroma!"

I'm not sure, but in the distance, I think I see the dark elf glance in my direction, although his face doesn't move. Hesitant, yet at the same time determined, I make my way closer. I'm certain my eyes aren't deceiving me. I call out again, "Gilroma!"

It seems like he doesn't hear me until his body turns slightly.

I make contact with his glowing yellow eyes. There is something hidden in his expression. Before I can work out what it is, he moves past the dark elf and disappears around the corner of the mountain.

- CHAPTER FIVE -

I run toward the spot Gilroma stood only moments before. The unknown elf stares at me, his eyes dark and wanting to dive deep into my soul. I prepare for battle, pushing aside my curiosity over where Gilroma went as well as my puzzlement of how I lost Harut. I don't understand why Gilroma was talking to this dark elf, but I'm sure if I ask him, he will have a good reason. I'm also sure that even if I ask the dark elf nicely, he still won't tell me what they were talking about. So I brace my emotions and gather my focus with each step that I take.

Suddenly, the dark elf waves his hands quickly in large circles, then he shoves his hands out at me. Magic explodes from his fingertips, slams straight into me, and knocks me to the ground. The impact jars my body from my backside up to my spine and my neck. My head throbs, and my backside aches from the impact. I brush my palms on my pants and gather my strength to scramble to a standing position.

I take a deep breath and try to focus on the dark elf only to find him gone. He has vanished. I thought he would stay around and battle me. Feeling confused, I scamper forward, searching for Gilroma. The last time I saw him, he darted around the corner of the mountainside.

Kara? Kara, where are you? Elan's voice speaks to me telepathically.

"I'm here, Elan, behind the big mountain."

Oh, dragon scales! Thank the talons! I couldn't see you anywhere. Elan's voice is full of concentration as though she's looking for me.

"Sorry. I went to chase Harut, but then I ran into Gilroma. Can you come and get me? I think we should face the battle together."

Of course. Seconds later, Elan crests the mountain and circles me before she lands. I climb onto her back and don my dragon-scale cloak, pulling the hood over my head. Elan turns invisible, and I instantly feel a hundred times safer.

Why are you around here?

"Freya asked me to find Harut, and I followed him around the mountain only to find Gilroma talking to a dark elf. I went to talk with Gilroma, but he disappeared around the side of the mountain. And now I can't find him. Can you help me?"

Of course. She pushes off the ground and flaps her wings, lifting us into the air. *From what you said, it's rather strange behavior. And you say Harut was around here?*

"He went this way, but I can't see him."

I can't smell him around here, but perhaps the stench of angels of death fills my nose. The smell of corpses isn't pleasant, and it seems stuck in my nostrils.

"I know what you mean. But don't you think you'd be able to smell it around here too?"

Elan flies to the corner of the mountain then around the next corner until, eventually, we are back on a battlefield. There is no sign of Gilroma or Harut. An uneasiness crawls through my stomach, and I'm getting the feeling that something isn't right. I frown then shake it off. I'm being ridiculous. The battle is setting my nerves on edge, and everything seems to be turning into something that it's not. I stroke Elan's scales then stick my hand under one at the edge of the saddle. "Any sign of Eir?"

Elan's voice leaks with pain. *No. I'm sorry.*

My heart sinks. "I'm getting worried. Let's go fight this battle so we can finish it earlier. I really want to start looking for her."

Elan flies up then dives straight into the battle, aiming directly at some dark elves. I tug out my bow and nock an arrow, pulling the string taut. I direct it straight at a dark elf, and the shaft imbeds into his chest. He collapses to his knees and falls face-first onto the ground, unmoving. I notice several dark elves turn to look at the dark elf then up at the sky in the direction the arrow traveled from. The arrow has alerted them of my presence. I'm still glad invisibility is a shock that I can hold over others in a fight.

I nock another arrow, aim it straight for another dark elf, then let it fly. It sings sweetly as it slices the air, heading straight for the dark elf's heart. I clench my fist, clasping on to the hope that it will stay true. As it nears, my excitement rises but is then crushed when the arrow hits something invisible and drops to the ground.

"Oh, Vanir! They've put up barriers already."

Elan sweeps and changes direction as I catch sight of an auburn glow among the fighters. My heart lifts with excitement and anticipation. I study the figure then yelp with joy when I spot the spiky red hair of Hildr. I jump up and down on the saddle. "She's back from Anita's ward. She must've recovered enough to come and fight again."

She swings her sword with ease and dedication. When she gets close to a dark elf, she places her hand directly on the elf and jolts her with magic. The dark elf collapses to her knees. Hildr swings her sword and removes the dark elf's head then moves on to the next one. Her face is taut with excitement as she revels in the thrill of the fight.

"That's the Hildr I know."

A soft rumble sounds through Elan's throat. *That certainly is. She is a little rock, that one.*

Elan circles and dives down, breathing fire on the group of elves. She roars a sound full of frustration when the fire bounces off their magic barriers. *Dragon scales! These elves are using their magic too much. It's making it hard for us to get through to them. Even with two of our warriors against one of theirs, it is barely an even battle. There are so few of you that have the magic.*

A loud roar sounds from behind us, and at first, I think it is Drogon or Tanda, but the wrong color appears in the corner of my eye.

Far behind me, a dragon approaches, and my cheeks turn clammy with excitement. It is a yellow dragon. I hope this is Loki finally bringing his army of dragons to rescue Asgard. Behind the yellow dragon is an array of about sixty different dragons flying in our direction.

"It's Loki's army."

Is it? Elan sounds surprised. *So where's Loki?*

- CHAPTER SIX -

The big yellow dragon flies our way. It definitely looks like the yellow dragon that was in Loki's army, but it's not Loki sitting on its back. It's not even one of the dwarf giants. The dwarf giants are sitting on the other dragons but not this one. I stare at the figure sitting in the saddle and lean in closer. Glowing yellow eyes stare at me from under a bald head and a face full of spiky tattoos.

"Gilroma?" The word is an astonished mutter from my lips.

Aha, Elan says. *I wasn't sure if I could trust him before. Do you think we can trust him? Because a whole army is coming our way, and it's full of dragons.*

"I believe we can trust him. Gilroma's done nothing to betray me. Except that is not his army—it's Loki's. I swear it is. Only Loki has an army made up of dragons and dwarf giants."

Gilroma stares intensely at me, and I think I read amusement on his face. I lift my hand to wave, but he suddenly changes direction, nose-diving toward the battlefield. My heartbeat speeds up, hoping that he is rushing to help our side and protect the Valkyries from the dark elves. The yellow dragon swoops down and shoots out a large plume of fire. Except it is aimed straight at the Valkyries and lands on a large group of angels of death. Corpses are a bad enough smell, but the intensity increases with the smell of burning corpses. Their wings sizzle, and their bodies disintegrate, creating a potent odor as they turn to ash right before us.

"No," I say in a horrified whisper. "What is going on, Elan? He's supposed to be on our side."

Is he? Elan doesn't bother to hide the sarcasm in her voice. *It sure doesn't look like it, and I'm pretty sure he just proved which side he is on. Now I understand why I couldn't bring myself to trust him. We have to stop this now.*

She flicks her tail, maneuvering us to face the other direction, and aims for the first dragon coming our way. She aims straight for the rider, purposely avoiding the dragon. Before I have a chance to pull out my bow and nock an arrow, she is within a dragon's length away, too close. I lower my hood and pull my sword from behind my back. Elan is still invisible, so the rider would only be able to see my face and the weapons—not a big target for them to focus on. At the last second, she flaps, taking me higher, away from the battle. I look down, searching for my target, and find him swinging from Elan's talons. Muffled screams reach my ears.

The dragon looks confused as it glances over its shoulder, finding its back empty. Elan's body wobbles, and she wriggles then flings the giant off in the other direction. His body crashes to the ground, where he lies, unmoving. The dragon flips in time to watch its rider falling in the opposite direction. Something registers on the dragon's face, and suddenly, it nose-dives toward Tanda.

Tanda flies over the top of the battlefield, oblivious to the dragon charging her way. "Elan, you need to warn Tanda."

Already done.

It is hard to believe her as I watch Tanda showing the approaching dragon no attention. I worry my lip. "This is not good. The dragons attacking don't know that they were part of your clan. They should want to come back and join the rest of the dragons."

They should. But the dragons don't know any better. They were born into this clan that Loki has made without knowing that they came from a better tribe living in the wastelands. All they have known is what Loki wanted them to see. It breaks my heart to think that they're going to be our enemies. Loki has a lot to answer for. Her voice is layered with spite and malice.

As I watch the dragon approach Tanda, I wonder again what happened to Loki.

"Elan, I'm so confused. Why is Gilroma leading the army when it's Loki's army? It doesn't make sense."

I understand, Kara. But it's simple. You've been betrayed. Someone you thought was working for your best interest wasn't.

My mind analyzes how exactly I managed to become acquainted with Gilroma. It takes a while, but I realize it was Anita who sent me to him. My shoulders slump as I contemplate the possibility that she may be on his side. Then I shake my head. She's a wingless Valkyrie that represents Asgard. She has served our academy and healed the students, including my friends. She's probably treating Naga at this very moment.

As we fly, my heart breaks over the betrayal to Asgard and me. Surely sweet, caring Anita hasn't been a part of this war attempting to bring down Asgard. I know she received the unfair treatment of being a wingless Valkyrie like us, but I find it hard to believe that she would betray us. Then again, it wasn't long ago that I thought the same about Harut and Gilroma, who is now attacking angels of death and the Valkyries.

I don't know who to believe or what to think. I toss my head to the side and groan, catching sight of Hildr's red hair glowing in the sun. She is still fighting well and manages to withstand anything that comes near her, either by magical force or the sword. Britta is doing much the same. They're not the best fighters in the field, but they know enough to keep themselves alive. Seeing them makes me think of Eir, and it saddens me to know that these three have supported me all the way through and would fight with me to the end.

Elan's body shakes underneath me, and my mind travels to her mother, brother, and all the dragons in the wastelands. Earning their trust took some work, but it was worth it. They have supported me in working on our union with the dragons and improving how we interact with each other. They have also helped me prove my worth as a Valkyrie to Asgard, even though I don't have wings. Elan's golden wings catch my eye. Except I do have wings. Elan's wings are instruments to be used as though they are my own. Her wings are more impressive than those of the Valkyries. These thoughts lift my spirits, and I find the will to keep going.

Spotting the diving yellow dragon brings my attention back to the battle. Tanda flies within its sights, appearing not to notice her pursuer. Suddenly, when the dragon is almost upon her, Tanda maneuvers sideways and flips, knocking the dragon with her big hump. I gasp, and my mouth drops open in shock. I've never seen a move like that before.

Elan giggles. *Tanda's been working on that move.*

I tap my dragon friend lightly on the back. "You didn't tell me that."

I've been keeping it a secret, she says nonchalantly.

"That's an unusual move but clearly effective." The enemy dragon was flung straight into the ground, where it roars in pain, its wing broken.

She's been practicing that just in case something like this happened. We don't want to fight the dragons. We hope that we can talk them through this. But we will hurt them if we have to. These dragons have no emotional attachment to us because they don't know that we are their family. It's harder for us, knowing that these dragons came from our parents' eggs.

"Clever thinking. At least you thought ahead. Clearly, I've been way too trusting."

Don't be too hard on yourself, Kara. That is one of the main things that makes me want to be your friend. You have a big heart and one that believes the best in everyone.

As I ponder her words, a yellow flash erupts in the corner of my eye, and I turn to see the yellow dragon heading straight for us.

- CHAPTER SEVEN -

As the glaring yellow eyes of my magic mentor stare at me with disdain, dread overpowers me. This is my mentor. My skills are only at a beginner's level, and he knows it. He knows my every move. Combined with this knowledge is that he is the one I placed my trust in. He is someone who came to my aid on many occasions. I can't believe he's pursuing me with the intent of harm.

Elan spots him coming our way, and she turns. Even though my cloak of invisibility shields me, my face and weapons show, and Gilroma knows what to look for. I curse myself for not putting my weapons away and hiding my face better, although I need to see what's going on in the battle, so I don't know how I could've effectively hidden my face. Besides, I know Gilroma can sense my magic, so hiding better probably wouldn't make a difference. As I stare at the glowing yellow eyes, I can't help but reprimand myself. I should have been more guarded when I met him. I shouldn't have been so open with him, even if Anita did direct me to him. I'm too trusting.

As though hearing my thoughts, Elan speaks, *Don't be so hard on yourself. You're young. These are part of the lessons of being young.*

"So are you, yet you are wise."

I'm young in years, but a dragon matures faster than Valkyries, and I have been brought up in the dragon wastelands. It teaches many lessons you can't learn in a controlled environment. She pauses. I guess it's like someone who has grown up without a home and has to learn to live life day-to-day and face danger without being killed.

My spirits lift with her words, but worry still nibbles at me. "What am I supposed to do with Gilroma? His magic far outweighs mine. I haven't even begun to touch the tip of the iceberg."

Suddenly, the dark emblem that I saw on the first day in his little cave springs to my mind. That symbol meant, "I am one with the darkness." Gilroma was always one with the darkness—he just didn't show it, not to me. Mentally, I kick myself over and over, jerking in the saddle as I fight the urge to carry through with my abuse physically.

Believe in yourself, Kara. I believe in you. Otherwise, I wouldn't have joined you and agree to bond with you. Mother saw it too. That's why she had me watching you. We will fight them together.

"Thanks, Elan. Whatever happens, I've loved having you by my side."

You say that like this is our last moment together. Don't worry. There will be plenty of more days to come.

"I hope you're right." I suck in a deep breath, opening my lungs to their full capacity, and let it out. I repeat the process, trying to calm my nerves. I don't let my eyes leave Gilroma. The magic wells deep inside of me, and I feel it burning, demanding to be released.

My hand tingles with magic, and I absentmindedly reach for the hilt of my trusty sword, which I had plunged deep into the giant that Elan and I killed on our first battle together. I let it rest across the front of my saddle, and my fingers stroke the wings on the hilt. It is such a strange yet thoughtful design that Rota added to it. It's almost as though she was giving me my wings—wings that I will never physically have—except I don't need my own wings anymore. I have Elan's.

My magic tingles as my fingers caress the wings on the hilt. My imagination conjures an image of those wings flying. An impossible feat, yet it still manages to bring a smile to my face. It would be a great thing to happen. Briefly, I touch the wings of the sword hilt with both hands until I realize that Gilroma is only a few feet away. A sudden urge strikes me, and I fling my arm back and thrust the sword forward, directing it tip first with my magic. It aims straight for Gilroma, and I'm amazed at my ability to do something I haven't practiced.

As the sword approaches him, I curse that I was too chicken to aim straight for his heart. Something deep inside still hopes that there is a good reason he is riding a dragon that's fighting against Asgard. I curse myself for being so naive and trusting. Having a good side seems to leave me open to everyone.

The sword nears Gilroma, aiming for his shoulder. It's going to hurt and disable him. The aim is true until suddenly he forces his magic at the sword and flings it in the opposite direction. Disheartened, I watch it project farther away from me, making me wish I knew how to call to my sword. I could certainly use it.

A gloating smile spreads across Gilroma's face, and he waves his hands in my direction. Suddenly, a force hits me, ripping at my coat with an intensity that flings my arms back and my cloak off.

"There. Now the world can see you. No more hiding behind the invisibility scales of your dragon."

Dragon scales! Elan curses. She suddenly swerves, jerking my body with her as she dives and flips around until we hit something. Gilroma looks shocked as his dragon is knocked to the side, yet he manages to regain some of the control.

"It is a shame I can't do the same to your dragon," he says. "It's not fair that she can hide behind her invisibility." He thrusts his hand at me, shooting out magic.

I counteract swiftly, blocking it. Sweat trickles down my forehead. The worry of the fight is getting to me. Elan dives underneath Gilroma's dragon, flips upside down, and seconds later, the dragon roars.

We flip again, and I glance back to see blood trickling from the dragon's stomach. Elan must've dragged her claws over the dragon's scales in the opposite direction. The yellow dragon bares its teeth and looks directly at me, as does Gilroma.

Instinctively, my hand reaches up to the necklace he gave me recently. It jolts, and my hand closes around it for a second. A patch of gold catches my eye, and I spot my dragon-scale cloak lying helplessly on the ground. I wish this necklace could turn me invisible and put a barrier around Elan and me while I'm on her back. Then I wouldn't have to concentrate on protection against every attack.

At the same time, a stench of burning corpses reaches me, and I glimpse at the army below and in the skies. Many angels of death are burning to dust, incinerated by the dragons from Loki's army. I spot Freya. Her face is contorted in mourning for the loss of her angels of death.

Another red-and-yellow glow catches my eye, and I see a large fireball heading toward a Valkyrie that looks very much like Mist. It's hard to tell at this distance, though, because the winged Valkyries look so similar. But at the last second, before the fire hits, she twists and clasps a lock of blond hair, twirling it in her fingers, a trait of Mist's when she's uncertain or contemplating something. An expression of horror plasters across her face right before she bursts into flames. Her beautiful white feathers singe to a crisp and fall to the ground along with the embers containing her flesh.

A flash of brown careens up toward the dragon that unleashed its plume of fire at Mist. Drogon aims straight for the dragon's belly with his amply horned head then throws his head back, scraping it along the dragon's stomach in the opposite direction of its scales. A horn plunges deep into the dragon's flesh, and the dragon bellows a roar. Drogon retracts his horn and flips his body, flinging his spiked tail into the side of the dragon. Quickly, he pulls his tail back and dives in the opposite direction before the dragon can recover enough to pursue him. It suddenly makes sense why Drogon has so many horns on his head and tail compared to the other dragons

"Where did you go?" I hear Gilroma's voice calling.

Suddenly I remember I'm sitting in the air on Elan's back. I gaze at the glowing yellow eyes, wondering how I didn't think they were creepy before. He searches the area where I was only moments before as though he can't see me.

"How did you do that?" he asks. "You can't do anything that I didn't teach you."

At first, I am confused. Why can't he see me? Then I remember I was holding my necklace and willed to be invisible. Judging by the way Gilroma is looking at me, it must have worked.

Elan hovers then moves above the spot where Gilroma searches. He continues to look, appearing more frustrated with each passing moment. "Where are you?" he asks again.

"Why are you doing this, Gilroma?"

His eyes flick in my direction, and he instantly shoots magic. Elan dives, causing the magic to miss us.

"Why are you fighting against Asgard?" I ask again. "I took you in as a friend. I trusted you. Now I find out you are an enemy of Asgard and me, and now you're trying to kill me."

"Don't you see?" His gruff voice is laced with spite. "Asgard is never going to accept me. I've had to live in hiding for years."

"I understand Asgard is closed-minded. But I'm working on that, remember? My efforts aren't completely hopeless. And when it works, you can come out of hiding."

"Don't be ridiculous. Asgard will never accept me, just like they will never accept you."

"I always believe there's hope."

"And that's where you're wrong." He sneers. "You are just as bad as Anita. I thought Anita would be on our side because she is wingless and strong-willed. I thought she would turn against Asgard. She was against all these rules that Odin had for his Valkyries. But she didn't. She went through so many things, as you've been through, and both of you still fight for Asgard. You are stupid women."

Although I know I have lost a friend, my heart rejoices to hear that Anita hasn't joined him. I had hoped that her heart was as good as I thought.

Suddenly Gilroma flicks his hands, and out of nowhere, several daggers fly out of his saddle and aim straight for me. He can't see me, but there are so many daggers, I wouldn't be surprised if a few of them hit me.

- CHAPTER EIGHT -

Elan suddenly maneuvers in a different direction, but she is too late. A dagger slams into my side, and I cry out in pain. When I wished on my necklace, I had hoped that, along with turning invisible, I would have placed a protective barrier around me as well. But these daggers are made with elven magic and can pierce through all magic barriers.

For that, you'll die. Elan flips and whacks the dragon with her tail while flying sideways. My body jerks, and it's a struggle to hang on and pull my mind away from the pain. As we spin, I catch a glimpse of what is happening below. I must get down there. It isn't looking good. It looked bad before, but now it's a slaughter against Asgard. If we don't stop this or get help, then Asgard will fall.

An explosion sounds, and I turn my head in time to see a mountain collapse onto Asgard's surface. The whole mountain disappears into the crust.

Is this another sign of the end of Asgard and the prediction of Ragnarök? This can't be. Fear is taking over, creeping its way into my brain and interfering with my mindset.

No. I can't let this happen. I grit my teeth, yank out the dagger lodged in my side, and send it flying back at Gilroma. It pierces straight back into his side, and he cries out in pain. A smile creeps across my face—it's a small accomplishment. The dagger pierces straight through his magic as well. He shimmers before my eyes, his form blurring in and out until he eventually stabilizes and remains in the form of Loki.

My eyes bulge with shock. "Gilroma is Loki!"

"What? You're surprised?" Loki asks through gasps. "Did you forget that I can turn into any shape I like?"

Elan flips and stares straight at our attacker. *I knew something was off with him.* A rumble sounds in her throat. *Let me have a piece of him. There is so much he should pay for, especially for what he did to the dragons.*

Something silver catches my eye. I glance at it, only to see my sword. The wings on the hilt have sprouted and are flapping back to me. I must've charmed them when my fingers were ladened with magic and I stroked them. I didn't even mean to. I'm so glad it came back. I grasp the hilt of the sword, and the wings pack themselves away, turning back into the solid silver wings that resemble emblems.

A roar echoes through the valley, and I spin around. A horde of dragons approaches from the side of the Valkyrie academy. I gaze at them in horror. These are the dragons that the Valkyries have used as fighting targets and have mistreated from the beginning. My face loses all feeling. I hope they aren't coming to attack the Valkyries as well. I wouldn't blame them if they did, but we can't afford any more enemies. I cling to hope that Eingana managed to visit them and convince them to be on our side, but I haven't heard if she had any success.

Another cry comes from the other direction. Fearing that this is the sound of our side falling apart over the approaching dragons, I turn, only to find Loki arching backward and crying out in pain. I notice a dagger protruding from his back. I gaze behind him and spot white wings, and I'm surprised to see Mistress Sigrun several feet away.

She catches my eye and shrugs. "You let your guard down again, Kara. Besides, I was returning the dagger to its rightful owner." She smirks and dives back to the ground, screaming the Valkyrie war cry.

I don't know what to think. Mistress Sigrun saved me again, and she called me by my name.

The yellow dragon aims for Elan's throat. She darts sideways, giving me another full view of the untamed dragons approaching. Their faces are full of anger and hostility.

"Oh, Elan. Please tell me that your mother has talked to these dragons and convinced them to join our side."

The brown dragon in front roars, and my throat turns dry.

Don't worry. I've been talking to them, and I've had a good chat with them as well. I convinced them to be on this side despite the winged Valkyries' mistreatment. I just held a conversation with the one in front that roared. He said that Naga convinced Anita to go into the stalls and unlock all the chains. Naga was reinforcing their commitment to Asgard as Anita set them free. I'm pretty sure they are here to help.

I jig with joy in my saddle. "Yay! At least that's some good news."

But that's not the only good news.

I pause, trying to contain my excitement. "What do you mean?"

Look behind you.

I look over my shoulder. In the distance, the sky is filled with dragons coming straight from the dragon wastelands. Leading them are three dragons with glimmering golden scales. They can be none other than Eingana, Sobek, and Elan's sister.

Mother is bringing all the dragons from the wasteland. And yes, they are fighting on our side. Hopefully, they can convince these other dragons not to attack. It will be tearing them up inside that they may have to fight against their children.

Another cry erupts from behind me, and I spin around to see Loki arching backward again.

"You let your guard down again, Kara!" Mistress Sigrun hovers behind him, and Rota joins her. "We'll have to work on your alertness once we get out of this mess." They fly in, clasp Loki by his arms on either side, and pull him from his dragon.

With heartfelt gratitude, I say, "Thank you. It's probably best if you take him away from here before the dragons arrive. Something tells me that they might want a piece of him, and I mean that literally."

An evil grin crosses the mistress's face. "Then maybe we should leave him here." Suddenly, Loki transforms, and between the two Valkyries is Harut.

"No!" The word escapes from my lips in hushed horror. "You're supposed to be my friend."

"I am your friend, Kara. Help me escape these Valkyries. Two against one who is injured is not fair." He flaps his wings then grimaces.

My heart sinks at a rapid rate. I can't believe that this is another friend I placed my trust in. I trusted him to my very core. He helped me in Midgard. He defended me when I was in the camp of the angels of death. He was always kind to me and made me feel special. It breaks my heart from all sides, but I shake my head. "No. My friends don't fight against my realm and conspire to bring it down."

The look on his face pulls at my heartstrings. It is a pinnacle of sadness. The deep-brown eyes turn down at the corners. I have to keep reminding myself that this is Loki, who is also the deceitful Gilroma and zmey. The thief that stole the dragon eggs to build an army to fight against Asgard. This is not a friend of mine.

My thoughts and emotional turmoil are interrupted.

"Oh, for Asgard's sake!" Mistress Sigrun screws up her nose. "Change back into Loki. You stink."

- CHAPTER NINE -

"I think we need to take this little bonehead to see Odin. He can face his punishment there. Oath brother or not." Mistress Sigrun jerks at Harut's arm, causing him to wince in pain as they drag him toward the palace.

Elan cruises next to them for a while, giving them protection from the yellow dragon Loki was riding earlier.

Suddenly remembering where I am after being shocked by Loki turning into Harut, I glimpse around at the dwarf giants. They have stopped attacking the fighters below and hover in the air, watching the dragons approach. Half of their army faces the dragons from the academy, and the other half faces the dragons on the horizon that are approaching from the wastelands.

I can only imagine what is going through the heads of Elan's clan. I would hate to be in their shoes and have to fight against my own kind, knowing they could be my offspring. The yellow dragon continues to annoy us, and Elan's patience grows thin.

If this dragon doesn't leave me alone soon, I'm going to do something worse than I already have. She circles Mistress Sigrun and Rota as they fly Loki back to the palace. Every so often, she twitches and bares her teeth at the yellow dragon's throat when it flies too close. Then she flicks her tail at the dragon's legs.

It's a rough ride, but I've spent endless hours on her back, so it's nothing I haven't trained for. At this moment, I am incredibly grateful that I spent the time making the saddle and the additional strap to tie around my waist, securing me in place.

The breeze tugs at my hair, whipping it around my face and making it hard to see. Each time I flick my head in the opposite direction to push it behind me, the leather on the saddle creaks and groans. This intensifies when the other dragon recuperates from the attack Elan has bestowed upon it.

The yellow dragon's eyes are set on rescuing Loki. Elan bellows a roar, sending shivers right to my core, and she snaps so aggressively that I need to hang on even though I'm strapped in. The force of her movement flings my head to the side and jerks my body as she grabs the dragon within her talons, ripping them along its scales. She then flips and jams her horns into the scales, piercing the soft skin underneath.

Flicking out her wings, she halts abruptly then shoots to the top of the dragon and clasps its wings with her talons. Then she kicks and tears holes in the membrane flesh and knocks the yellow dragon hard to the ground. The dragon flutters its wings in a useless motion as the air sails through the gaps. The dragon careens in a half-controlled fall to the ground.

That ought to do it. Elan watches the dragon fall. *Although it breaks my heart to do so.* Her shoulders sag, and I can almost feel her pain as she stares at the dragon she has hurt.

I pet her underneath her scales just at the edge of the saddle. "I know, Elan. It's heartbreaking that they were raised like this. They don't know any better."

With the other dragon gone, Mistress Sigrun and Rota land safely on the palace grounds and drag the worried-looking Loki into the palace.

The newly arrived dragons surround the battlefield in the sky, and a fight begins between the dwarf giants' dragons and the dragons of Asgard. The dwarf giants drag their swords and weapons up the scales of the other dragons, slicing up their scales.

With Eingana leading the charge, the dragons of the wastelands hesitantly attack, until they realize they don't have a choice. A few dwarf giants are flung off the dragons and fall to their death. Others are ripped from their saddles and chomped in half. It's a bloody mess, with each side having casualties.

The dwarf giants use a wide range of weapons, including swords, spears, arrows, and even morning stars they bludgeon into the dragon's sides. Roars of pain bellow from each side of the battlefield, and plumes of fire shoot in all directions. Both sides suffer significant wounds, and dragons are flopping to the ground in defeat. It's clear that Loki's dragons have had more practice in battle and in learning how to fight against each other, but Eingana has more dragons, and the fights are often two or three against one. It's a battle that I wouldn't want to be in the middle of.

Elan remains out of the primary dragon battle, keeping me out of the harm. We concentrate on the battlefield on the ground and on helping the Valkyries and the angels of death.

Freya spots Mistress Sigrun and Rota returning, and she runs to the palace. I wouldn't be surprised if she knew Harut's secret identity. If she doesn't already know, I'm sure she has her suspicions.

I spot Prima below. She is fighting without reprieve, taking on the enemy. Her past wounds are healed. I will always be thankful for the fast healing powers of the Valkyrie.

Prima darts sideways, and a large form narrowly misses her. A giant has fallen from the sky, and his head smashes against a rock. His dragon roars and tears at another dragon above. As much as I hate the scene, I'm thankful that another enemy is removed from the sky. The dragons continue the fight until the wings of Loki's dragon are twisted and bent in the wrong direction. We watch as it follows its rider to the ground.

Britta and Hildr work together against the chief elf. Each one uses her magic against him and blocks his magic when he shoots in their direction. They dodge the weapons he throws even though their barriers are up. They must have learned that the elven weapons would pierce straight through them.

I watch, fascinated, as Britta skips to the left, then to the right, then to the center, jabbing her hand at the chief dark elf and shooting magic into his side. Every time she has a chance, she darts in until she catches him off guard and knocks him to the ground.

As Britta leans over the top of the chief elf, making him succumb, Hildr charges toward her, runs up her back, and jumps, slamming her sword into the center of the dark elf's chest.

His body convulses a couple of times until his eyes turn glassy.

A bright light explodes on the outskirts of the battle. I look in that direction, only to be shocked by what I see. The unconscious form of Eir lies on the sidelines. I blink, trying to clear my sight. I want to make sure I see things right before I let my heart fill with hope.

"Elan. Quick. Eir just appeared. I don't know how, although Britta and Hildr just defeated the chief dark elf." I point to Eir lying in the distance. "Perhaps she was trapped in the dark elf's magic after all."

Elan lands next to the spot where Eir lies. My breath is shallow, uncertain, as Elan squats. I'm so afraid to get my hopes up, hoping for her well-being. I jump off Elan's back, charge over to Eir, and press my fingers against her carotid artery.

"Thank Vanir! She still has a pulse." Finally, I allow some hope to creep into my heart. "Elan, can you help me get her to Anita?"

Absolutely! She clasps Eir tenderly in her talons, and I climb on my dragon's back. She pushes into the sky, aiming for the academy and our healer, Anita.

My heart fills with happiness, warming when I spot Hildr and Britta looking up and seeing Eir lying in Elan's talons. Elan flies low when she passes over the top of them, and I call down, "Good job, guys. She's alive, but her pulse is weak. We're taking her to Anita."

The excitement in their faces is evident. It's only a few moments before Elan lands on the academy grounds. I climb off her back, scoop Eir into my arms, and I'm about to carry her through the academy halls to see Anita when I spot Naga in a far corner. I rush over to him to find Anita squatting on his far side and working diligently on strapping one of Naga's legs.

Naga looks up. *Oh, thank Vanir!* The relief on Naga's face is unmistakable. *Naga so worried about Eir. Naga's happy to see her.* He nudges her quickly with his nose then turns to Anita. His big blue eyes are serious. *Is Eir all right?*

Anita strokes Naga's snout. "I hope so. I'll do my best." She turns to me. "Let's go."

- CHAPTER TEN -

I carry Eir down the academy corridor and place her on a gurney when we reach the healer's room. Anita observes her, opening her eyelids to check Eir's pupil responses before examining the rest of her body. "She's badly bruised. Otherwise, she seems fine except for being unconscious. She's hit her head hard. I can see the lump here." She points to a spot on Eir's head, where an egg-sized lump protrudes.

"She should be good. She looks to be healing already, just not enough to come back into consciousness."

I slump down onto a nearby chair. "Thank, Vanir!"

A large horn blares, and a wave of panic takes over my body. I hope this is not another invasion. I look at Anita with wide eyes. "What's that?"

"That's the horn of victory." Anita lets out a long breath. "That's a pleasant sound to hear." Her face fills with excitement, and my spirits lift.

"Really?"

She nods, a broad smile filling her face. "Really."

I charge out of the healer's room and down the corridor to Elan. "Elan. We won!"

Her golden-brown eyes widen with excitement. *Is that what that sound is?*

"That's what Anita says anyway." I climb up her back and sit in the saddle. "Let's go check it out."

Elan pushes up into the air and takes off back to the battlefield. All the dragons are on the ground, each accompanying one of the injured. Many dragons are hurt, with torn wings and pierced skin. The scene below us is devastating. Many injured Valkyries and angels of death lie among dark elves and dwarf giants who lie dead or wounded.

Gold flickers in the corner of my eye, piercing through the gloom.

Eingana hovers next to us. *We won. It's victory, but it's not sweet.*

Even though the war is finished, I feel a sadness overpower me as I gaze over the battlefield. "No. We've lost many on all sides. What caused it to stop?"

Loki was taken away, and the chief dark elf was killed. Because of that, I eventually managed to get through to the captain of these dragons. She believed me when I told her they were stolen from our clans.

"That's wonderful!" I gaze over to see Ness nuzzling Tanda, and my heart fills with joy. Finally, Mother is reunited with her daughter. Britta stands next to her, petting her scales, and Ness nudges her daughter's wingless Valkyrie friend as well. I can only imagine the conversation, and I smile. At least the battlefield is changing into a more relaxed and loving atmosphere.

Drogon prods Hildr. He has a small cut that Hildr is fussing over. Seeing the love between these dragons and their Valkyries brings joy to my heart.

A female voice speaks behind me. "You've done well, wingless." Even though the voice is familiar, it sounds strange because it's a voice I've known as being harsh, yet this time, there's a softness to it. Not only that, it's complimenting me.

I spin and face Mistress Sigrun. I blink, trying to wash away my disbelief. It looks like pride on her face. Next to her is Rota, who is covered in blood from the fight and beaming from ear to ear.

My mouth drops open, and I stumble over my words. "Th… thank you, Mistress."

The eyes of the academy leader travel from me and land on Eingana. She courteously nods her head. "Dragon."

"This is Eingana, Mistress. The leader of the dragons and the mother of Elan, my dragon."

Eingana lifts her head and stares down at the mistress. Her face looks intimidating, but the mistress doesn't back away.

"Nice to meet you, Eingana." The mistress nods her heads curiously again. "Thank you for your help."

You should be thanking Kara and her relationship with my daughter. It's because of Kara that we know where our eggs are disappearing to.

She has brought goodwill to the dragons. We wouldn't be here without Kara's influence.

A fleeting expression crosses the mistress's face, and for a moment, it looks like guilt. She looks at the ground. "I'm afraid that's true. It has taken her a long time to prove herself and for me to believe her. She has tried to prove herself many times without success, but today was a deal-breaker. Today, things change. We will no longer practice against the dragons." She grabs the dragon's tooth necklace around her neck, and her eyes narrow. She pulls it off. "I'll no longer wear this. It's not carrying the right symbol."

That's a good start, Eingana says, but her voice is still unconvinced. *And I would appreciate it if you stopped practice fighting against dragons. The way you set several Valkyries fighting against one dragon is unfair. It's uncalled for.*

Mistress Sigrun looks as though she's about to argue but holds her tongue. Her brows push together. I clench my teeth, thinking she is about to argue. Finally, she says, "It will no longer happen. In fact, after today, I shall be speaking with Odin." The mistress turns to me. "Which reminds me, Odin has asked for you."

The old dread rises in my stomach. Surely he doesn't want to punish me again. I've done so much for Asgard. Yet I hang on to hesitancy. I don't want to be yelled at again and told that I'm stupid. At the same time, I don't want to get my hopes up. The fleeting thought crosses my mind that perhaps this time, Odin will thank me rather than punish me. It takes an enormous amount of energy, but I push aside the dread and follow the mistress to the palace.

As I leave, Elan calls, You'll be fine. I'll see you when you get out.

The mistress and I enter the palace, and I follow her to Odin's hall. I distract myself by studying her majestic white wings. When we enter his throne room, he is sitting on his throne at the back of the hall. His face is set in a displeased expression, and two ravens sit on either side of him.

"Yes, yes. I know, Huginn and Muninn. I'm not completely blind." He brushes their beaks away from his ears. "I can see that Kara has arrived."

We stop in front of his throne, and he slowly climbs down and strolls toward us.

His eyebrow rises as he paces toward me. "So, young Kara, I believe."

My heart skips a beat. In the past, it's always been "wingless." I nod my head. "Yes, great Odin. My name is Kara."

"I have heard about your wondrous doings today, about how you brought the dragons together and captured the culprit. I believe you have been doing a great deal leading up to this battle. Because of you and your relationship with the dragons, you have prevented Ragnarök today."

My heart skips a beat. "Really?"

"Yes. I believe you have. We have many injured, including our wondrous warriors and Valkyries. Even Freya has lost many angels of death." He gestures to the corner, and for the first time, I see Freya sitting quietly. Her eyes are red and puffy, but she looks relieved that the fighting is over. "I have already thanked Freya for her help today. She said you called her. So again, you're to thank for that."

I bow my head slightly. "Thank you, great Odin. I appreciate it greatly."

"Because of what you've done for Asgard, you have proven your loyalty. For this, I have something to give you."

I blink and look at Odin with uncertainty.

Ignoring me, Odin continues. "I believe it'll be of great value to you." He moves toward me in silence. "Kneel," he demands.

I move down to my knees, one leg at a time, and gaze up to see a smug look on his face. He places a hand on my head. Something surges through me, and my body vibrates for a moment. "You have now been blessed with the reaping power of the winged Valkyries."

My mouth drops open, and I'm speechless.

He nods. "You have the power to reap souls for Ragnarök."

"Thank you, great Odin." I am humbled, and the shock makes it hard to speak, but my determination shines through. "I appreciate it greatly. But what about the other wingless Valkyries who fought today?"

Odin chuckles, and my mouth drops open. That is such an odd sound coming from him. "Yes, I will be passing out the power to them as well. But I wanted to change you first because you have worked harder toward this goal. Next, I will do your three friends, as they are the most observing. But in the future, I will no longer discriminate against the wingless Valkyries."

I almost spring to my feet and jump for joy. Finally, I have my victory.

A throat roughly clears in the corner, and I turn, spotting Mistress Sigrun staring earnestly at Odin.

"Oh, yes, yes. I know." Odin waves a hand dismissively at her then stares back at me. He holds out a hand.

I look questioningly at him then realize he's giving me a hand up. I clasp his hand, and he encloses it with his other hand before yanking me to my feet. "And one more thing." He releases my hand and glares at Mistress Sigrun. "I am breaking the alliance with the dragons."

I forget all the courtesies. "What? But they fought so well, and they fought on our side even though they were going up against their own babies."

"Yes, yes. I know this. That's why I'm breaking the alliance. I will no longer be demanding one of their young. As long as the dragons and Asgardians live in peace, they are free to roam the wastelands as they wish without giving up their offspring to us."

I squeal and jump up and down, clutching my hands. I am no longer able to contain myself. "Thank you, thank you, thank you, great Odin! I am so excited!" I stop jumping and stare at him. "Why are you telling me, though? Shouldn't you be telling the dragons?"

Odin smiles, and a raven lands on his shoulder. "I wanted you to tell them first. I think you deserve that pleasure. Yes, I will reinforce it afterward." He then flicks his hand at me dismissively. "Now run along. You've taken up too much of my time." He spins around and heads back to his throne as a servant enters the room with a big plate of food.

I begin to leave then pause to face Odin. "What will happen to Loki?"

Odin glares at me with his one eye then smiles. "Thor has returned from fighting the Midgard servant. He is taking Loki deep down into the earth, where stalactites hang from the ceiling and bats flutter. He mentioned something about binding him there with a venomous snake dropping burning poison onto his skin."

I screw up my nose. "That seems a bit harsh."

"So is attacking Asgard and betraying it. Blood oath brother or not," Odin says.

We reach the door, and he calls to me. "Oh, and make sure you rest. You'll need all of your energy for what's in store for you. Thor asked for your assistance."

The End

ACKNOWLEDGMENTS

I am touched by the enormous amount of support I have received from my immediate family. My husband has been a helpful first reader and at times been a wonderful motivator, with hints of ideas to help me through the blanks. The support from my three sons has also been overwhelming. They have put up with my head being in the clouds, thinking about the next plot twist or story for several years. Along with many hours spent working on my books and keeping in touch with my readers.

A big thank you to my extended family who support me being a book enthusiast.

A huge thank you to my editor, Neila Forssberg., her editing and writing tips, and my Proofreader, Kristina B., for picking up the things we missed.

Thank you to all of my readers who have loved my work, and continue to read my stories. I would love for you to share your thoughts in a review on one or all of the following:

Amazon.com

Goodreads

Barnes & Noble

You can follow Katrina Cope at:

https://www.facebook.com/Author.Katrina.Cope

https://twitter.com/Katrina_R_Cope

https://www.goodreads.com/author/show/7265107.Katrina_Cope

https://www.katrinacopebooks.com

http://http://www.amazon.com/Katrina-Cope/e/B00F00JF9M/

BOOKS BY KATRINA COPE

~~~~~

Pre-Teen Books

THE SANCTUM SERIES

JAYDEN'S CYBERMOUNTAIN
SCARLET'S ESCAPE
TAYLOR'S PLIGHT
ERIC & THE BLACK AXES
ADRIANNA'S SURGE

~~~~~

Young Adult Urban Fantasy

AFTERLIFE SERIES

FLEDGLING
THE TAKING
ANGELIC RETRIBUTION
DIVIDED PATHS
<u>Afterlife Novelette</u>
THE GATEKEEPER

~~~~~

Young Adult Urban Paranormal Fantasy
~~~~~

SUPERNATURAL EVOLVEMENT SERIES

(Associated with the Afterlife Series)
WITCH'S LEGACY (#0.5 Prequel)
AALIYAH

~~~~~

Young Adult Fantasy Nordic Myths

VALKYRIE ACADEMY DRAGON ALLIANCE

SERIES

MARKED (Prequel)
CHOSEN
VANISHED
SCORNED
INFLICTED
EMPOWERED
AMBUSHED
WARNED
ABDUCTED
BESIEGED
DECEIVED
~~~~~

DID YOU ENJOY THIS BOOK?
YOU CAN MAKE A BIG DIFFERENCE.

Honest reviews of my books help bring them to the attention of other readers.

If you've enjoyed this book, I'd be grateful if you could spend a few minutes leaving a review (it can be as short as you like).
The review can be left on Amazon and Goodreads.
Thank you very much.

ABOUT THE AUTHOR

Katrina is an author of several Young Adult and Preteen/Middle Grade novels. Each of her released books reaching the top 100 in certain categories on the Amazon's Best Sellers Rank – a few even as high as number one.

She resides in Queensland, Australia. Her three teenage boys and husband for over nineteen years treat her like a princess. Unfortunately though, this princess still has to do domestic chores.

From a very young age, she has been a very creative person and has spent many years travelling the world and observing many different personalities and cultures. Her favourite personalities have been the strange ones, yet the ones under the radar also hold a place in her heart.

During her last extensive travels, she spent 16 nights in a bomb shelter on a Kibbutz 8 kilometers off the Lebanese border. It was to avoid Katyusha bombs that the resident volunteers decided to name her after (she is still trying to work out why).

Katrina's online home is at
www.katrinacopebooks.com

You can connect with Katrina on:

Twitter https://twitter.com/Katrina_R_Cope

Facebook

https://www.facebook.com/Author.Katrina.Cope

Instagram

https://www.instagram.com/katrina_cope_author

Pinterest

https://www.pinterest.com.au/katrinacope56

Email authorkatrinacope@gmail.com

9 780648 661399